His Sugar Baby Princess

A Possessive Age Gap Instalove Novella

Rose richards

I0694093

TWISTED ROSE
+PUBLISHING+

Copyright © 2026 by Rose Richards

All rights reserved.

No part of this publication may be reproduced, distributed, or transmitted in any form or by any means, including photocopying, recording, or other electronic or mechanical methods, without the prior written permission of the publisher, except as permitted by U.S. copyright law.

The story, all names, characters, and incidents portrayed in this production are fictitious. No identification with actual persons (living or deceased), places, buildings, and products is intended or should be inferred.

Paperback ISBN: 978-1-960162-44-1

Book Cover by Avery Daisy Book Design

Contents

Chapter 1

I STARE AT MY bank account on my phone screen. Sixty-three dollars until my next paycheck, and rent is due in five days.

Sixty-three dollars. I could stretch that if I skipped coffee and walked everywhere and maybe stopped eating. Who am I kidding? That might buy me food, but I'd still be short for rent. The numbers blur and I blink hard. I refuse to cry.

"Ugh," I mutter, dropping my phone onto my bed like it personally betrayed me.

My best friend Ella is at my apartment for a study session, and she looks up from her textbook. "That bad?"

"Yep. I don't know how I'm going to make rent this month. Again." I flop backward onto my pillows. "Maybe I should drop out and become a barista full-time."

Ella bites her lip, and I can see she's debating something. "Okay, don't freak out, but I have an idea."

I prop myself up on my elbows. "If you're about to suggest I sell my eggs or a kidney, I'm listening."

She laughs. "Nothing that dramatic. There's this website—it's totally legit. For companionship. You'd be arm candy at events for wealthy people who need a date. Galas, business dinners. No sex required." She pulls up a website on her phone. "See? Very professional."

I scroll through. The women on it are gorgeous—model-level gorgeous with bodies that belong in fitness ads, and hair that probably costs more to maintain than my entire monthly grocery budget.

"El, I don't know... These women look like they stepped out of Vogue. I look like I stepped out of a thrift store."

"Whatever, Jen. You're beautiful. And smart and charming. You'd be perfect." She gives me a pointed look. "And you need the money."

She's not wrong about that last part. I look back at my phone where the sixty-three dollars is still mocking me.

Twenty minutes later, I've created a profile that says I'm a college student, communications major, well-spoken, comfortable in formal settings—I almost snort when I write that part. I can fake it, right? I've never been to a gala in my life. My idea of formal is wearing jeans without holes in them.

I upload the best photo I have and hit submit before I can overthink it.

Ugh, what am I doing? Some rich guy is going to look at my photo next to those women and laugh. "Communications major seeks financial stability" doesn't exactly scream "worth thousands of dollars." I'm going to get zero responses and feel like an idiot for even trying.

"There," I say, showing Ella. "Done. Nothing will probably come of it anyway."

Famous last words.

By the next morning, I have seven inquiries. Seven. I stare at my phone in disbelief as I walk to my 9 a.m. class.

Most are for dinner dates or corporate events with decent pay. But one message stands out.

Someone named K. Locke. It's a full-day booking for a charity gala this Saturday. Includes shopping for appropriate attire, hair and makeup, and attendance at an evening event. He's offering $15,000.

I stop walking in the middle of the sidewalk. Someone bumps into me and mutters something rude, but I don't care.

Fifteen thousand dollars.

That's... that's six months of rent. Groceries and textbooks and maybe even a night out where I don't have to calculate whether I can afford an appetizer. I could breathe for the first time in three years.

Hands shaking, I type back: *I'm interested. What would this entail exactly?*

His response comes within minutes: *Coffee meeting first. Tomorrow, 10 a.m.? I'll send you the address.*

I should ask more questions. I should be cautious. I should probably run this by someone who isn't as desperate as I am.

But fifteen thousand dollars.

I type: *I'll be there.*

Then stare at the sent message like it might bite me. What am I doing?

The café is in the classy part of town where I definitely don't belong. I arrive ten minutes early because I'm anxious like that, wearing my best jeans and the jean jacket I've had since freshman year of high school. The cuff is fraying. I noticed it this morning and tried to trim the loose threads, but apparently I'm not as crafty as I thought because I made it worse.

I tug at my sleeve and glance around. Everyone here looks rich. Cashmere sweaters and designer bags and the kind of calm that comes from never worrying about overdraft fees. I have sixty-three dollars—well, fifty-eight now after buying the latte I definitely shouldn't have bought.

Cool. This is fine.

My leg bounces under the table. What am I doing? Meeting a stranger who's offering me an insane amount of money to be his date? This is how horror movies start. Or those true crime podcasts Ella listens to. *She was last seen at an upscale café, wearing a jean jacket she'd had since high school...*

But fifteen thousand dollars.

I'm stirring my overpriced latte when the door opens, and I glance up out of habit.

And forget how to breathe.

The man walking in is tall—well over six feet—with brown hair going silver at the temples and blue-gray eyes that sweep the room like he's cataloging everything in it. His suit fits like it was sewn onto his body. He moves like he owns the place. Hell, he might own the place.

No way that's K. Locke.

Men who look like that don't need to pay for dates. They have women throwing themselves at them. If it is him, he'll take one look at me in my thrift store jacket with the frayed cuff and walk right back out.

His eyes land on me, and he smiles.

Oh god, it is him.

He approaches. "Jennifer?"

His voice is deep with a roughness that sends heat pooling between my legs. I'm suddenly very aware that I'm wearing my old cotton underwear with the stretched-out elastic, because they're growing damp.

This is a business meeting. Get it together.

I nod because words are apparently beyond me.

"Kevin Locke." He extends his hand, and when I take it, his grip is firm and warm and oh fuck, I'm blushing. His hand completely engulfs mine. Swallows it. His thumb brushes across my knuckle and I feel it deep in my core.

Is my palm sweating? It feels like my palm is sweating. He's going to think I'm disgusting. I should pull away. I don't.

"I've heard that name before," I manage, trying to place it.

"Probably from the business section of the news if you read it," he says with a slight smile. "I'm in real estate development. Commercial properties, mostly."

He's beautiful. Can men be beautiful? Those silver temples and that jaw and the way his shoulders fill out that jacket. Jesus. I need to get it together before I start drooling.

"Thank you for meeting me," he says. He still hasn't dropped my hand.

"Of course," I say, attempting to sound like a normal human who meets attractive older men for coffee all the time. "Thanks for the opportunity."

He releases my hand slowly, his fingers trailing across my palm in a way that leaves my skin tingling. He sits across from me and I try not to stare. Even the way he sits is sexy—relaxed but alert, legs spread, taking up space like he's entitled to it.

He hasn't looked away from my face, and I grab my latte to avoid fidgeting. His gaze drops to my mouth, watching my lips on the rim of the cup.

Heat flickers in his expression. Just for a second.

Oh. Oh wow.

I set the cup down too fast and it clatters against the saucer. Real smooth, Jennifer. Very sophisticated. Very "comfortable in formal settings."

"Nervous?" he asks, and his tone sounds pleased.

"A little," I admit. "I've never done anything like this before."

"Good."

Good? What does that mean? Is he relieved I'm not a professional? Or does he like that I'm nervous? And why does the idea of him liking my nervousness send a weird little flip through me?

"Tell me about yourself," he says, resting his forearms on the table. The fabric of his shirt stretches across his shoulders and I forget what words are.

He smells incredible—cedar and amber. The kind of cologne that makes you want to bury your face in someone's neck and breathe it in.

Whoa. Where did that come from? Focus.

"I'm a junior at State," I say. "Communications major, marketing minor. Hoping to go into PR after graduation."

"Why PR?" He's watching me intently, like my answer actually matters. Like I'm not just some broke college kid in a fraying jacket.

"I like the challenge of it. Taking something complicated and making people care about it. Finding the story that connects." I'm rambling. I always ramble when I'm nervous. "Plus, I'm good at talking to people. Usually. When I'm not completely tongue-tied."

His mouth curves up, and oh god, he has a dimple. Just one, on the left side. It's devastating. It's not fair. He already had the jaw and the shoulders and the voice, and now there's a dimple too?

"You're doing fine," he says, and his voice drops lower. "Better than fine."

Heat floods my face. I take another sip of my latte so I don't have to respond.

"What about your family?" he asks.

The familiar ache settles in my chest. "My parents died three years ago in a car accident. So yes, I'm doing this because I'm broke, not because it's some glamorous side hustle."

I don't know why I'm being so blunt. Maybe because there's no point in pretending. He's going to find out who I really am eventually. Might as well be now.

His expression softens. "I'm sorry. That must have been incredibly difficult."

"It was. It is." I shrug, trying to play it off like I always do. "But I'm managing. Obviously barely, given that I'm here. But I'm still in school, so that's something."

He's quiet for a moment, and I wonder if I just tanked my chances by being too honest about how pathetic my life is.

Then he says, "Can I tell you why I'm on that website?"

I nod, curious.

"I'm tired of women who want me for my money or my connections. Every date becomes a performance—they're auditioning to be Mrs. Locke, angling for access to my world." He runs his hand through his hair, and I watch the silver catch the light. "I wanted something honest. Transactional, yes, but at least I'd know exactly what someone wanted from me. No hidden agendas."

"That sounds lonely," I say softly.

"It is." His eyes meet mine. "But then I saw your profile, and it felt different. Genuine. Most people try to make their life sound more exciting."

"I made it sound a little more glamorous than it really is. There's nothing exciting about checking your bank account before buying a coffee and knowing you shouldn't, but still buying it anyway because you need the caffeine to function."

Desire pools low in my belly at the sound of his laugh. It's warm. Authentic. I want to make him do it again.

Shit. Why is my body going haywire around him? He's paying me to be his date. This is a job interview. I need to stop imagining what his hands would feel like on—

Nope. Not going there.

"All right, Jennifer. Here's what I need." He shifts closer, and I catch another wave of his cologne, and my brain short-circuits all over again. "I have a charity gala Saturday night. It's important for my business, lots of networking, lots of conversations with people I'd rather not spend time with. I need someone who can handle themselves in that environment. Someone intelligent, charming, who won't be intimidated by wealth or status."

"And you think that's me?" I ask, genuinely surprised.

I'm sitting here in a jacket that's seen better days, and he thinks I can handle a room full of rich people?

His gaze travels over my face slowly, lingering on my mouth. "I know it is."

The certainty in his voice makes my pulse skip. He just met me—how can he be so sure? I'm nothing like those women on the website, nothing like whoever he usually dates.

"The day starts with shopping," he continues. "You'll need a gown, shoes, jewelry—everything. Then hair and makeup. The gala starts at seven and usually runs until eleven. I'll introduce you to people. You'll smile, make conversation, be charming." His eyes lock on mine. "Think you can do that?"

"Yes." The word comes out breathier than I intended.

"Good." He pulls out his phone. "What's your number?"

I recite it, and he adds me to his contacts. A moment later, my phone buzzes.

Kevin: Saturday, 10 a.m. Wear something comfortable. We'll be shopping for a while.

I look up from my phone to find him watching me with that intense focus that makes me feel like I'm the only person in the room.

"Fifteen thousand dollars," I say, just to confirm I didn't hallucinate this entire conversation. "For one day."

"For your time and your company." He stands. The meeting is apparently over. "The shopping is on top of the money. Everything you need will be provided."

I stand too, and he's so much taller than me that I have to tilt my head back to meet his eyes. From here I can see the shadow of stubble along his jaw. What would it feel like under my fingers? What would he do if I reached out and touched it?

Jesus. What is wrong with me?

"I'll see you Saturday, Jennifer." He extends his hand again, and when I take it, he holds on a moment longer than necessary. His thumb traces a slow circle on my skin. His gaze drops to where our hands are joined, and possessiveness flickers across his face.

My breath catches in my throat.

But before I can say or do anything stupid, he releases me and walks away.

I stand there like an idiot long after he's gone. The spot where he touched me still tingles. I'm buzzing all over, and I don't know if it's the caffeine or the man or the fifteen thousand dollars or some combination of all three.

What the hell just happened?

Chapter 2

I SPEND THE NEXT three days obsessing and telling my-self it's nerves about the gala. Anyone would feel the same way, knowing they're about to be surrounded by wealthy people in a world they don't belong to. And making fifteen thousand dollars in a single day. That's a normal thing to be nervous about.

That's a lie, though. I'm obsessing about him. The way he looked, how I forgot to breathe when his hand swallowed mine. That dimple. The way his voice dropped when he said my name.

Ugh, I've got it bad for a hot older guy who is hiring me for one day. One day. And then I'll never see him again, and this will all feel like a dream.

I wake up early on Saturday and take the time to shower and shave everywhere. I know this isn't a date date where we'll end up in bed together. Since my parents died, I've barely had time to breathe, let alone date—which is why I'm still a virgin. Some hand stuff and one mediocre blow job in the back of a car during junior year doesn't exactly prepare you for whatever a real date looks like.

Not that this job is a real date.

I stand in front of my closet for twenty minutes trying to figure out what "something comfortable" means. Comfortable for me is yoga pants and a ratty t-shirt, but I'm guessing that's not what he had in mind. I settle on black leggings and a flowing cream-colored blouse that hides the fact that my stomach isn't perfectly flat. I leave my hair down in loose waves because every time I try to style it, it looks worse.

When I'm ready, I stare at myself in the mirror and wonder why he picked me. The mirror doesn't show me anything special. Just a cute college girl with anxiety and split ends.

At 9:58, my phone buzzes.

Kevin: I'm downstairs.

As I grab my purse and head out, my heart pounds with each step down the stairs. This is just shopping. With a man who makes me forget how to form sentences. No big deal.

When I push through the building's front door, I stop dead.

There's a sleek black car parked at the curb, and Kevin is leaning against it like he stepped out of a magazine. Dark jeans hug his thighs, and his crisp white button-down has the sleeves rolled up to show off his forearms. Who knew forearms could be attractive? Apparently I do now.

His gaze finds me immediately, traveling down my body and back up in a slow sweep that makes my skin prickle.

"Morning," he says.

I walk toward him on unsteady legs. "Morning." Shit, did that sound squeaky? I think it did.

He opens the passenger door for me, and I catch his scent as I slide past him—that cedar and amber, even better than I remembered. I have to fight the urge to turn my face into his chest and breathe deeply.

The car's interior is butter-soft leather. I sink into the seat and try not to think about how out of place I am. A broke college girl in a rich man's car, about to be dressed up like a doll for a party.

Is that what this is? Am I a doll he's dressing up?

He closes my door and slides into the driver's seat, and suddenly the space feels smaller. Like he's taking up all the oxygen.

"Sleep well?" he asks, pulling into traffic.

"Not really," I admit. "I was nervous."

"About today?"

"About everything."

He glances at me, and his expression is warm. "Don't be nervous. It's just shopping."

Right. Shopping with a man who makes my pulse race by existing. He's going to drop money on me like it's nothing, in stores I'd never dare walk into on my own.

"Tell me about your week," he says. "How were classes?"

I tell him about my disaster of a group project where half the team isn't pulling their weight. About my professor who I'm convinced hates me because I asked too many questions. About the paper I have due in a week that I haven't started yet because I've been too busy obsessing over today.

He asks follow-up questions, laughs at all the right moments. I almost forget to be nervous. Then his fingers brush my knee.

It's an accident. It has to be.

"Sorry," he murmurs, but he shifts gears again, returning his hand to the wheel.

Every nerve ending in my body is suddenly focused on that one spot of contact. I sit frozen like an idiot, trying to remember how to breathe normally while heat spreads up my thigh from where he touched me.

Holy fuck. This is going to be a very long day.

I'm quiet until we pull up to a boutique with a French name I can't pronounce and window displays that scream "if you have to ask the price, you can't afford it."

"Kevin, I don't think—" I start as soon as he cuts the engine.

"Trust me," he interrupts gently. "Sit for a moment, and I'll get the door for you."

As he walks around the car, I watch him and remind myself again this isn't a real date. He's not the man for me. He's paying me to play a role, and after tonight, I'll go back to my ramen noodles and normal life.

Why does watching him open my door make my chest ache?

He offers me his hand. The moment his palm engulfs mine, that electric feeling is back—the same jolt I felt at the café. He helps me out but doesn't let go. His fingers lace through mine.

His gaze drops to my mouth, and the air between us crackles with electricity.

When a car horn blares behind us, the spell breaks. He releases my hand and places his palm on my lower back, guiding me toward the boutique entrance.

I can feel the heat of him through my thin blouse. Each finger pressing against my spine. My body wants to lean into his touch, which is insane because I don't even know this man, not really.

A woman appears the moment we walk in. "Mr. Locke, it's wonderful to see you again."

Again.

He's brought women here before. The thought bothers me more than it should. It's ridiculous that it bothers me at all. I have no claim on him. None.

"Margaret, this is Jennifer. We need a gown for tonight's gala." His hand is still on my lower back, warm and possessive. "Something elegant but memorable."

Margaret gives me a practiced once-over. I resist the urge to suck in my stomach. "I have several pieces that would be ideal. What's your size, dear?"

I tell her, hating how the number sounds out loud, and she disappears into the back.

"Relax," Kevin murmurs, his lips close to my ear. His breath tickles my neck. "You're gorgeous. Everything will look stunning on you."

My face heats. "You don't have to say that."

"I'm not saying it to be nice." His palm slides to my hip, and he turns me to face him. We're standing so close I have to tilt my head up to meet his eyes. "I'm saying it because it's true. You're beautiful, Jennifer. Surely you know that."

I don't know what to say. I know I'm cute. Passably attractive on a good day. But he's looking at me like no one ever has, like I'm worth the attention.

Margaret returns with an armful of dresses before I can respond. "Let's start with these," she says, leading me toward a dressing room.

The first dress is navy with a plunging neckline that shows more skin than I usually risk. I put it on and stare at myself in the mirror. The cut is gorgeous, even if I wish I had bigger breasts to fill it. Still...not bad.

I step out onto the platform in front of the three-way mirror, fighting the urge to cross my arms over my chest. Kevin is sitting in a chair facing the platform, legs spread, forearms resting on his thighs.

His eyes go dark.

But all I can think is that he's seeing every flaw. The way my stomach isn't flat. The soft parts I usually hide under oversized sweaters. I don't belong in a dress like this. I belong in—

"Turn around," he says, his voice rough.

I do, slowly, watching his reflection in the mirror. His gaze travels over every inch of me, and I wonder what he sees. Is he comparing me to the other women he's brought here? Women who probably had personal trainers and expensive skincare routines and bodies that actually looked good in designer gowns.

"No," he says finally.

My heart sinks. "No? What's wrong with it?"

"Nothing's wrong with it. But it's not the one. Next."

Oh. Okay. Not a rejection of me. Just the dress.

The second dress is emerald green, strapless, with a fitted bodice that shows off my waist but also makes me hyper-aware of my curvy hips. When I step out, Kevin goes completely still.

"Fuck," he breathes.

"Good fuck or bad fuck?" I ask, using humor to hide how exposed I feel.

"Very good fuck." His eyes roam over me slowly. "But it's not quite right."

We go through three more dresses. His eyes rake over me hungrily with every change, but each time he shakes his head. Not quite right. And with each rejection, the voice in my head gets louder. He's going to realize this was a mistake.

Margaret brings out another dress, and my breath hitches.

It's a soft peach color, almost pink. The bodice is fitted and covered in delicate crystal embellishments that catch the light. The skirt flows like water, and I immediately imagine twirling in it and watching it billow around me.

I put it on, and when I look at myself in the mirror, I barely recognize the woman staring back.

She looks sophisticated. Put together. Like someone who belongs at a charity gala on the arm of a man like Kevin Locke's.

The illusion is going to crack any second. He's going to see through it.

I step out onto the platform, and Kevin's reaction is immediate. He stands abruptly and the chair scrapes against the floor. His hands clench at his sides like he's physically stopping himself from reaching for me.

"That's the one," he says, his voice barely above a growl. He walks toward me slowly, his gaze never leaving mine. "You look like a princess."

He's not saying it to mock me. It's reverent.

"A princess?" I manage, trying to sound teasing even though my heart feels like it's going to burst out of my chest.

"My princess." He reaches the platform and holds out his hand. When I take it, he brings my knuckles to his lips. The old-fashioned gesture makes warmth flutter in my chest. "That's what you are, Jennifer. My beautiful princess."

My princess. Mine.

The possessive edge combined with the sweetness of the words makes my knees go weak. I shouldn't like those two words so much. Princess. Mine.

Heat floods my cheeks. "I like Princess," I whisper.

His eyes glitter. "Good. Because I'm going to call you that a lot." His thumb brushes across my knuckles. "My princess. Mine to spoil."

Margaret appears with gold spiked heels. "Try these with it."

She leaves us alone again, and I slip on the heels. They add four inches to my height, but I'm still shorter than him.

I try walking in them, but I'm not used to heels this high. I take two steps and stumble.

Kevin catches me instantly.

We're suddenly inches apart. His large hands span my waist, fingers pressing into my sides through the thin fabric. I can feel the heat of his body. Smell his cologne.

His gaze drops to my mouth. "Careful," he murmurs, but he doesn't step back.

I should keep my distance. This is a job. This is—

I want to kiss him.

The thought arrives fully formed, and panic floods through me. What if he pulls away? What if he laughs? What if he gives me that polite smile people use when someone embarrasses themselves? He's going to think I'm some desperate girl who throws herself at older men—

Fuck it.

I go up on my toes and press my mouth to his.

For a split second, he freezes. My stomach plummets. I knew it. I'm an idiot. I'm going to have to spend the rest of the day with this man after I—

Then he groans, a low, desperate sound that I feel in my core. His hands tighten, and he takes over completely.

Oh. Not an idiot. Maybe.

He slides a hand up to cup my jaw, tilting my head to deepen the kiss. His other hand tangles in my hair. His mouth is hot and demanding, and when his tongue sweeps against my lower lip, I open for him without thinking.

I've been kissed before. Fumbling high school kisses. Sloppy frat party kisses. But this is different. He kisses me like he's trying to memorize the taste of me. Like he's writing his name on my soul.

His tongue slides against mine, and I make a sound somewhere between a whimper and a moan. He walks me backward until my back hits the mirror, pressing his body against mine.

He's hard. I can feel his cock through his jeans, pressed against my hip. Knowing I did that to him, that my kiss made this gorgeous, powerful man hard, makes me bold. I slide my hands up his chest. His muscles jump beneath his shirt, and he groans into my mouth.

Jesus. I'm making out with a man I barely know in a boutique dressing room. Anyone could walk in. Margaret could walk in. I should care. I don't. All that exists is the way he tastes, the way his hands claim my body, the desperate need for this to never stop.

He slides his hand from my jaw down my neck, pressing his thumb against my racing pulse. Then lower, skimming over the crystals on the bodice. When his palm curves around my breast, I inhale sharply.

"Fuck." He breaks the kiss and presses his forehead against mine. We're both breathing hard. "Jennifer, we can't. We're in public."

"I don't care," I whisper. I'm so turned on I can barely think. He could hike up this dress and take me right here against this mirror and I'd beg him not to stop.

"I care." His hand is still on my breast, his thumb brushing over my nipple through the fabric. Even through the layers,

I feel it everywhere. "Because when I get my hands on you properly, I want to take my time. I can't do that here."

When. Not if. When.

"I'm sorry," I say automatically. "I don't know why I—"

"Don't." His voice is sharp. "Don't apologize for that."

"But this isn't a date, and I just—"

"Jennifer." He holds my chin, forcing me to look at him. "I'm not sorry we kissed."

"You're not?"

"Not even a little bit." He brushes his thumb across my lower lip, and I shiver. "I've been thinking about kissing you since I walked into that café."

"Oh."

"Yeah. Oh." His smile turns predatory. "Now go change before I say fuck it and take you right here anyway."

Is that supposed to scare me? Because it's having the opposite effect.

My brain wars with my body as I retreat to the dressing room. Who the hell am I right now? Did I really just kiss him? In public? I'm either having a mental breakdown or a sexual awakening, and I honestly can't tell which.

Margaret comes for the dress, and I change back into my regular clothes. They feel wrong now. Too plain. Too ordinary. My body is still humming, and when I catch my reflection—hair messed up, lips swollen, cheeks flushed—I look like I've been thoroughly kissed.

When I emerge, Kevin is waiting with Margaret at the register. The dress is already in a garment bag.

His gaze tracks me as I approach, and the possessiveness in his expression makes my insides twist into knots of desire.

"All set," Margaret says cheerfully, handing Kevin a receipt. "You two make a stunning couple."

I open my mouth to correct her, but Kevin presses his palm against my spine, silencing me.

"Thank you, Margaret," he says smoothly. "We'll see you next time."

Next time. Like this is going to be a regular thing.

We walk to the car in silence, and I'm hyperaware of his touch guiding me. The warm weight of his hand. The way people glance at us as we pass—the gorgeous older man and the girl who clearly doesn't belong on his arm.

He opens the passenger door, and before I can slide in, he turns me to face him. His hand cups my jaw, tilting my face up, and then he kisses me again. Slower this time. Deeper. Like he's savoring me. Like he has all the time in the world.

When he pulls back, his voice is rough. "Get in the car before I forget we have more shopping to do."

My mind spins as I get in. I might be a virgin, but if tonight doesn't end with me in his bed, I'm going to be very disappointed.

Chapter 3

The shoe store is next, and Kevin sits beside me as I try on pair after pair. He rests his hand on the back of my chair, and every time I sit back, his fingers find the base of my neck. Drawing lazy circles on my skin.

I press my thighs together. Try to focus on the shoes.

"You're doing that on purpose," I accuse during one of those moments.

"Doing what?" He continues his maddening caress.

"That. The touching."

"I like touching you." His lips are close to my ear, his breath warm on my neck. "Is that a problem?"

"No," I whisper.

It's the opposite of a problem. It's making me so aroused I can barely remember what shoe size I wear.

"Good."

The salesperson returns with another box, and Kevin drops his hand like nothing happened. Like he wasn't making me wet in a public store. The moment we're alone again, his fingers return to my neck, tracing patterns that short-circuit my brain.

We settle on strappy gold heels that make my legs look longer but aren't so tall I'll fall on my face. Kevin pays without asking the price, and I try not to think about how much they cost.

At the jewelry store, he picks out pieces that make my resistance crumble—a delicate diamond necklace and matching earrings that catch the light like tiny stars.

"Kevin, it's too much," I protest weakly as the jeweler boxes everything up in velvet cases.

"Nothing is too much for you." He finds my hand and brings my knuckles to his lips again. The gesture makes my chest ache. "Let me spoil you, Jennifer. Please."

I want to argue. I want to tell him that I don't need diamonds, that I'd be happy with cubic zirconia, that he's already spent too much on me. But the way he looks at me, like giving me things brings him genuine joy, makes the words stick in my throat.

"Okay," I whisper, and warmth blooms in my chest at his smile.

But as we leave the jewelry store, a small voice in the back of my head whispers: What does he expect in return?

The thought makes me uncomfortable. Not because I don't want to give him anything—after that kiss in the boutique, I want to give him everything—but because I don't know what this is anymore. A transaction? A date?

When we get lunch at a café with cloth napkins, I automatically scan the menu for the cheapest item.

"Order what you actually want," Kevin says, watching me. "Not what you think you can afford."

I look up. "How did you—"

"You got that calculating look." His smile is gentle. "Jennifer, please. Order whatever sounds good."

Face heating, I order a salmon dish I'd never buy for myself, actively ignoring the mental math on how much ramen that would buy.

When the food comes, Kevin watches me eat with a satisfied expression that makes me self-conscious.

"What?" I ask, fork halfway to my mouth.

"Nothing. I like watching you enjoy yourself."

"That's not creepy at all," I tease.

"Maybe a little creepy," he admits, that devastating dimple appearing. "But you're irresistible when you're happy."

My throat tightens. "You can't keep saying stuff like that."

"Why not? It's true." He reaches across the table and takes my hand. "I think you have no idea how gorgeous you are, and that makes you even more captivating."

I don't know what to say. No one's ever talked to me like I'm special. No one's taken me to expensive lunches or bought me diamond necklaces or given me an entire afternoon of their attention.

I squeeze his hand because words feel inadequate.

He weaves his fingers through mine, and I realize I'm in serious trouble. The worst kind of trouble. I might actually fall for a man who's paying me to be his date. And I can't tell if this is real or if I'm just another girl he's charming before moving on.

The makeup counter is our next stop. Kevin stays close while the artist works, and I can see him in the mirror watching every brush stroke like he's memorizing the process.

"You have gorgeous bone structure," the artist says, tilting my chin toward the light. "And these eyes—wow. What I wouldn't give for lashes like this."

"She's stunning," Kevin agrees from behind us.

The artist catches my eye in the mirror and gives me a look that says girl, hold onto that one.

I wish I could explain that he's not mine. That after tonight, the carriage turns back into a pumpkin and I go back to being a college student, except now I'll be able to pay my rent for a few months.

When the artist finishes, I stare in the mirror. The smoky eyes make me look mysterious. Pink lips that look fuller, more kissable. I clean up nicely.

"Perfect," Kevin says, but he's watching me, not examining the makeup.

The artist shows me the products she used, and before I can even process the prices, Kevin is buying all of it.

"You don't have to—" I start.

"I want to." He slides his arm around my waist, pulling me against his side like it's the most natural thing in the world. "It gives me joy, and I like taking care of you."

The casual way he says it should alarm me. I've known this man for four days. Four days, and I feel safe in his arms and I'm hoping this doesn't end after tonight.

I want all of it.

"One more stop," he says as we leave the department store. "Hair."

The salon is intimidating with its white marble, fresh flowers, and stylists who look like they walked off a runway. Kevin's already made an appointment, because of course he has. The man clearly plans everything.

The stylist takes one look at my hair and starts talking about options. Updo, half-up, loose waves with volume.

"Whatever you think will look best," Kevin says. "I trust your judgment."

He checks his phone and frowns. His expression shifts—business mode clicking into place.

"I need to run back to the office," he says, tucking the phone away. "A work issue I have to handle. But take your time here. They'll call an Uber whenever you're ready." He pulls me close, his voice dropping low enough that only I can hear. "I'll pick you up at six-thirty. Think of me when you're putting on the dress."

Then he kisses me. Slow and deep, right there in the middle of the salon, in front of the stylists and the other clients and anyone else who might be watching.

When he pulls back, my brain has completely short-circuited.

"See you soon," he murmurs, and then he's gone.

Lips tingling, I sink into the salon chair.

"That man has it bad for you," the stylist says with a knowing smile.

"We just met," I protest weakly.

"Doesn't matter." She starts sectioning my hair. "I've been doing this for twenty years, and I know the look of a man who's completely gone for someone. You're a lucky woman."

Am I?

I spend the next three hours being pampered—hair styled into an elegant updo and mani/pedi painted a soft pink. And the whole time, I can't stop thinking.

He called me his. My princess. Mine to spoil.

Like this isn't only a one-day arrangement.

But it is. He's paying me fifteen thousand dollars to stand next to him and smile at rich people. That's the deal. Everything else—the kisses, the touching, the way he looks at me like I'm precious—that's just... what? Chemistry? Attraction? A rich man amusing himself with a college girl before moving on to someone in his own league?

I think about what he said at the café. About being tired of women who wanted him for his money or his connections. About wanting honesty.

Is this honest? I made a profile on a sugar baby website because I couldn't pay rent. I agreed to this because I was desperate. Does that make me any different from the women he was trying to avoid?

Guilt twists through me.

But I didn't kiss him because of his money. I kissed him because I couldn't not kiss him. Because he makes me feel reckless and makes me want things I've never wanted before.

What happens after tonight?

The question circles my brain as the stylist finishes my hair. As I tip generously with money Kevin left for me. As I climb into the Uber and watch the city slide past.

Maybe nothing happens. Maybe he takes me home, we have one incredible night, and then I never see him again. Maybe I'll be a story he tells—remember that girl from the website? The virgin who kissed me in a dressing room?

Wait. I haven't told him I'm a virgin.

I should probably tell him that...

Back at my tiny apartment, I find the garment bag and all the shopping bags already waiting by my door. Kevin must have had everything delivered while I was at the salon.

I let myself in and stand in my cramped living room, surrounded by bags that probably cost more than everything I own combined. The contrast is almost funny. Designer dress hanging on the door of a closet full of clearance rack finds. Diamond earrings sitting on a dresser I found on the curb.

I clean up carefully, making sure not to mess up my hair or smudge my makeup. Then I stand in my robe and stare at the dress.

I'm about to go to a charity gala with a man who makes my head spin. A man who kisses like he's trying to ruin me for anyone else. A man I want so badly it scares me.

And after the gala, I'm hoping to go home with him.

Hunger and anticipation claw through me, tangled with a feeling dangerously close to hope.

I put on my sexiest lingerie—pale pink lace that I bought on sale for a boyfriend who never got to see it. Then I step into the dress, carefully zipping it up and adjusting the bodice. The necklace settles against my collarbone. The earrings catch the light.

When I look in the mirror, I don't recognize the elegant, sophisticated woman staring back at me.

The illusion is fragile. I can feel it. One wrong word, one clumsy moment, and everyone will see through it. See the broke college girl playing dress-up.

But for tonight, maybe that's enough.

I practice walking in the heels until my phone buzzes at exactly six-thirty.

Kevin: I'm here.

I grab the clutch—also provided by Kevin—and head downstairs on trembling legs.

When I push through the building's front door, I stop dead.

There's a black town car with an actual driver waiting at the curb. And Kevin is standing beside it in a tuxedo.

Holy shit.

If I thought he was attractive before, I was wrong. The black jacket fits him perfectly, emphasizing his broad shoulders and trim waist. His hair is styled back, showing off his jaw. He looks like he stepped off a movie set.

When he sees me, he goes completely still. Then he's crossing the distance between us, pulling me into his arms.

"Christ," he breathes against my hair. "You're absolutely stunning."

"You're not so bad yourself," I manage, and he laughs.

"Not so bad?" He pulls back enough to look at me, one eyebrow raised. "I think you can do better than that."

"You take my breath away," I whisper, and I mean it. I really, really mean it.

Fierceness flashes in his expression. "Good. Because you've been taking mine since the moment I saw you."

He kisses me. Slow and sensual, his hand cradling the back of my head so he doesn't mess up my hair. The consideration in the middle of the passion makes my chest ache.

When we break apart, I'm practically vibrating.

"We need to go," he says, but he doesn't sound happy about it. "Before I say fuck the gala and take you upstairs."

I shiver. Part of me wants to tell him to do exactly that.

He helps me into the car. The moment we're settled in the back seat, he puts the privacy screen up between us and the driver, and pulls me against his side. I fit perfectly in the curve of his body.

"I couldn't stop thinking about you," he murmurs against my hair.

Raw neediness pulses through me. "Then maybe you shouldn't have been such a gentleman."

"Trust me, I'm regretting it." His fingers tighten on my shoulder. "Being a gentleman is taking considerable effort right now. I keep thinking about how you kissed me."

My cheeks warm at the reminder. "I can't believe I did that. I'm not usually so... bold."

"I love that you took what you wanted." His lips brush my temple, and when his palm settles on my thigh, I can't breathe for a second. "It made me want to give you everything."

"What if we skipped it?" The words come out before I can stop them. "The gala, I mean."

"God." He groans, his fingers tightening on my thigh. "I wish we could. But we have to make an appearance first."

"How long do we have to stay?" I can hear how breathless I sound. Like I'm counting down the minutes.

"As long as it takes to make the necessary rounds. Then I'm taking you home with me."

Home. His home.

I'm going to sleep with him tonight. This gorgeous, older, completely-out-of-my-league man is going to take me to his home and—

"Okay," I whisper.

He pulls back enough to look at me. "Okay?"

Say it. Be bold. Take what you want.

"Yes. I want to go home with you."

I sound like I know what I'm doing. Like I've done this before. Like I'm not a twenty-one-year-old virgin who's only given one terrible blowjob in her entire life.

I should tell him. I should definitely tell him.

He makes a sound low in his throat—almost a growl—and kisses me again. Deep and desperate, like he's been waiting all day for this. I kiss him back, trying to match his intensity, hoping he can't feel how hard my heart is pounding.

When we finally break apart, his gaze is dark with desire, and I know I look equally wrecked.

Yeah. I'm not telling him I'm a virgin.

What if he doesn't want to deal with someone who has no idea what she's doing? What if he wants experienced? What if—

He kisses me again, deep and claiming, and I stop spiraling. I'll figure it out. How hard can it be?

"You're killing me," he mutters, adjusting his tie.

I giggle nervously and try to compose myself.

The car slows, and I look out the window to see a historic building lit up like it belongs in a fairy tale. Photographers line the entrance. Everyone I can see is wearing formal wear.

Kevin squeezes my hand. "Ready?"

No. Not even a little bit.

"Yes," I say anyway.

He helps me out of the car, and cameras flash as we walk toward the entrance together. His hand is warm and steady on my lower back, and I try to look like I belong here. And try not to trip and face-plant in front of everyone.

Fake it till you make it. You're a princess tonight. His princess.

Even if it's only for one night.

Chapter 4

THE VENUE IS OVERWHELMING with its crystal chandeliers and polished marble floors. Everywhere I look there's wealth on display. The women are all in designer gowns dripping with jewels, and the men in elegant tuxedos.

I don't belong here.

Kevin takes my arm, and when I peek up at him, he's looking at me like I'm the only person in the room. Like everyone else is background noise. It helps. A little.

We make it through the necessary introductions—business partners with firm handshakes, investors who look me over like they're appraising an acquisition, a couple who immediately wants me to talk to their daughter about a marketing intern job. Each time, Kevin introduces me with this note of pride in his voice that makes my chest warm.

I'm nodding along to a group of women discussing the foundation's work—a clean water initiative in developing countries—when Kevin leans down to murmur in my ear.

"I need to speak with someone about business. Will you be okay for a few minutes?"

"Of course," I say, even though the idea of being alone in this room full of strangers makes my palms sweat. Everyone here knows each other.

"I'll be right back."

I watch him walk away, admiring how good he looks in that tux, when a new voice beside me makes me jump.

"If I were Kevin, I wouldn't leave you by yourself."

I turn to find a man in his early forties. He's handsome in that calculated, too-polished way, with a smile that doesn't reach his eyes. He's holding two champagne flutes.

"Harrison Mercer," he introduces himself, offering me one of the glasses. "And you must be Kevin's companion for the evening."

The way he says companion makes my skin crawl.

I take the champagne because refusing seems rude. "Jennifer Martinez."

"Lovely to meet you, Jennifer." His gaze traveling over me feels invasive. "Tell me, how long have you known our dear Kevin?"

"Not long," I admit, taking a sip to cover my nervousness.

"Ah." He steps closer, and I resist the urge to back away. "Kevin's a generous man. Very generous. With his time, his money, his attention." A pause. "For a while, anyway."

For a while.

My stomach drops as I think of how smooth Kevin was at the café. How easily he charmed me. How he said all the right things, made all the right gestures. How many women has he sat across from in that exact spot, saying those exact words?

Stop it. Harrison is trying to get in your head.

But the seed is planted.

"I'm sure I don't know what you mean," I manage, but my voice comes out wrong. Thin.

"Of course you don't." His smile widens. "Would you like to dance?" he asks. "Since Kevin has abandoned you."

I don't want to dance with this man. Everything about him sets off alarm bells—the way he's standing too close, the way his gaze keeps dropping to my cleavage, the way he's clearly enjoying making me uncomfortable.

But people are watching. And I don't know how to say no without causing a scene.

"I suppose one dance wouldn't hurt."

He takes my champagne and sets both flutes on a passing waiter's tray, then leads me onto the dance floor. His hand settles too low on my waist. He holds me too close.

"You're quite stunning," he says as we move to the music. "I can see why Kevin selected you."

Selected. Like I'm an item he picked off a shelf.

Though that is a little like what happened, isn't it? I made a profile. He chose me. I'm here because he's paying me fifteen thousand dollars.

"When you find yourself looking for new... opportunities..." Harrison continues, his breath too warm on my face. He slides a business card into my palm, fingers lingering too long. "Give me a call."

I'm about to tell him exactly where he can shove his business card when a hand grips Harrison's shoulder and yanks him backward.

"Get your fucking hands off her."

Kevin's voice is low and dangerous in a way I've never heard before.

Harrison steps back, hands raised in mock surrender. "Hey, just being friendly, Locke."

"Get the fuck away from her." Each word is clipped. "And if I see you near her again, we're going to have a problem."

"Always so possessive." Harrison's focus flicks to me. "Enjoy it while it lasts, Jennifer."

He walks away, and I'm left standing there with Kevin, who looks like he wants to commit murder.

"Are you okay?" He turns to me, and his whole demeanor shifts—the rage is still there but banked now, replaced by concern. His hands cup my face, tilting it up so he can search my expression. "Did he hurt you?"

"No, I'm fine. Just…" I hold up the business card. "Apparently I need a backup plan for when you get bored of me."

The words come out light, teasing. But I'm not really joking. I want to know.

His expression is fierce. "Come with me. Now."

He takes my hand and pulls me through the crowd toward the balcony doors. Several people try to stop him for conversation, but he ignores them all, focused entirely on getting us alone.

The balcony is blessedly empty and cooler than the crowded ballroom. City lights sparkle below us like scattered diamonds, and I can finally breathe properly.

Kevin paces for a moment, running his hand through his hair and messing up the careful styling, before turning to face me.

"Harrison Mercer is a piece of shit who's been trying to undermine me for years. Whatever he said to you, it was designed to get under my skin."

"So it's not true?" I ask. "You don't have a pattern of dropping women?"

Please say no. Please tell me I'm not the latest in a long line of girls you've charmed and discarded.

"No." He closes the distance between us, and suddenly I'm backed against the railing with his hands gripping the stone on either side of me. Caging me in. "I've dated, yes. But nothing serious. Nothing that mattered." That dark intensity bores into me. "And I've never felt like this before."

"Like what?"

"Like I'm losing my fucking mind." He presses his forehead against mine, and I can feel his breath, warm and unsteady. "I can't think straight when you're near me. I can't breathe right. All I can think about is touching you, tasting you, making you mine."

My heart slams against my ribs. "Kevin—"

"I know it's crazy." His voice is raw. Urgent. "But I can't shake this feeling that I've been waiting for you without even knowing it."

It's too much. Too fast. Too intense.

And exactly what I want to hear.

"I feel it too," I whisper. "This pull."

His sharp intake of breath tells me that was the right thing to say.

"Tell me what Harrison said to you," he says. "All of it."

"That you date beautiful young things for a month or two, then you move on." I force myself to meet his gaze.

His voice is fierce. Absolute. "I'm not looking to move on from you, Jennifer. I'm looking to—" He stops himself.

"Looking to what?"

"Keep you."

The words hang between us. Honest and terrifying.

"I know that sounds insane," he continues. "I know I have no right to say that when we barely know each other. But the thought of you with someone else, of Harrison or any other man touching you..." His hands tighten on the railing. "It makes me want to break things."

Holy fuck.

The possessive tone in his voice should scare me. Instead, heat pools between my legs. I'm already wet, and he hasn't even touched me yet.

"I don't want anyone else," I say softly. "I only want you."

"Fuck," he growls, and then he's kissing me.

His hands tangle in my hair as he presses my back against the railing. The cold stone bites through my dress, but I don't care. I kiss him back desperately, fisting my hands in his jacket, pulling him closer.

His tongue sweeps into my mouth and I moan. Too loud. Probably audible to anyone who might be inside. But I can't bring myself to care. Not when he's kissing me like I'm air and he's been drowning.

He cups my breasts through the dress and I can't hold back a whimper. God, I want him to pull the fabric down and touch me properly. I want his hands everywhere.

"I've been dying to touch you all night," he groans against my lips. "I saw all the men watching you in there, and I wanted to tell them all that you're mine."

Wait. Men were watching me?

A new kind of power I've never felt before stirs in my chest. I might not know what I'm doing, but this gorgeous, successful, completely-out-of-my-league man is desperate for me. And apparently I was turning heads I didn't even notice.

"I'm yours," I murmur. "At least right now."

"Right now," he agrees, but his tone suggests he wants more than right now. He pulls up one of my legs and I wrap it around his hip, grinding against him without thinking.

We're on a balcony. At a charity gala. Anyone could walk out here.

"Fuck, Jennifer. We're in public," he groans, but his mouth is on my neck now, sucking gently on the sensitive skin below my ear.

"I don't care." And I don't. That's the terrifying part. I'm so turned on I can barely think straight. All I want is his hands on me.

"I care," he murmurs against my throat, "because when I'm inside you, it's not going to be gentle or quiet."

My head spins. I barely process what's happening before he's bunched up part of my dress between us—a poof of peach fabric—and his hand is sliding between my legs.

His fingers brush against my panties, and even through the fabric, the sensation makes me jolt.

"Christ, you're wet."

"I've been wet since this morning," I admit. My voice doesn't sound like mine. Too breathless. Too needy.

He snaps and slips his fingers under the lace, and when he finds me completely bare, he makes a sound like I've physically wounded him.

"Fuck," he breathes. One finger glides through my folds, and I have to bite my lip to keep from crying out. "Is this all for me?"

"Yes." I rock against his hand, chasing the sensation. "All for you."

He circles my clit, and pleasure shoots through me like lightning.

I've touched myself before. Late at night, under the covers, thinking about faceless men and half-formed fantasies. But this is completely different. I don't know what he's going to do next. I can't anticipate, can't control. And the uncertainty is intoxicating.

Is this normal? Or is it because it's him?

"That's it," he encourages as I rock against his hand faster. "Take what you need."

I'm shameless. Grinding against his fingers in public. I should care about getting caught, or what people would think if they saw us.

I don't care about anything but him.

"Are you going to come for me?" he murmurs against my ear.

"Yes," I whimper. "Please, Kevin, I need—"

He eases one finger inside me, and I cry out before I can stop myself. He's gentle—so gentle—circling my clit with his thumb while he slowly fucks me with his finger.

The pleasure builds and I'm rocking against him furiously. Oh, god. I'm going to come.

"So tight," he groans. "You're going to feel amazing around my cock."

The dirty talk combined with his fingers is too much. I shatter, muffling my cry against his shoulder as pleasure explodes through every nerve ending. My whole body shakes as he works me through it, gentling his touch as I come down.

"You're fucking beautiful when you come," he whispers.

I'm floating in a happy place and thoughts feel like too much. I'm still catching my breath when I hear voices from inside. Someone's approaching the balcony doors.

Kevin withdraws his hand quickly, smoothing down my dress. Then he brings his fingers to his mouth and licks them clean, never breaking eye contact with me.

Holy shit. That's the hottest thing I've ever seen.

"We should go back inside," he says. His voice is rough. Strained.

I nod, too breathless to reply, and let him lead me back into the ballroom.

I'm hyperaware of every eye on us. Can they tell? Can they see how flushed I am, how shaky my legs are, how swollen my lips are from kissing? Do they know what happened on that balcony?

Kevin keeps me close for the rest of the evening. His hand never leaves my body. Each touch is possessive. Claiming.

We make it through dinner, but I barely taste the expensive food. Kevin has his hand on my thigh under the table, drawing maddening patterns through the fabric of my dress. During the speeches, he traces his fingers along the inside of my wrist, and even that innocent touch feels electric.

By the time we've made all the necessary appearances, I'm wound so tight I might actually go crazy.

"I've done my duty," Kevin says, brushing his lips against my ear. "Ready to get out of here?"

"God, yes."

He makes quick goodbyes, cutting off conversations politely. Several people try to stop us, but he's clearly a man on a mission. Within minutes, we're outside, and the car is waiting.

The moment we're inside with the privacy screen up, Kevin pulls me onto his lap.

"Come here," he growls, and then his mouth is on mine.

This time I'm not nervous. I'm greedy.

I straddle him, dress riding up around my hips, and grind against the hardness I can feel through his pants. The version of me from this morning—the one who was scared to order an expensive lunch—would be horrified.

Current me doesn't care.

He pushes the dress higher, hands sliding up my thighs, and when his fingers brush the edge of my panties, I rock against him shamelessly.

"Fuck," he groans. "You're still wet."

"I told you. I've been wet all day."

He slips his fingers under the lace, finding me slick and swollen. "Christ, Jennifer. I'm not sure I can wait until I get you home."

"I need you," I whimper, grinding against his hand. "Please."

He circles my clit, building the pressure, and I moan against his mouth. "Don't tempt me. Not yet. Not here." But he doesn't stop touching me. "I'll make you come again first. Would you like that?"

"Yes."

He slides two fingers inside me, and the stretch makes me gasp. It's more than before—a sharp, delicious pressure that makes my toes curl.

I go wild on his fingers. Grinding, rolling my hips, experimenting with angles to find what feels best. The car feels like a private universe as the city lights slide past the windows and the interior fills with the obscene wet sounds of him finger-fucking me.

"That's it," he encourages. "Come for me again, sweetheart. Show me how much you need me."

When he adds a third finger, I whimper from pleasure.

If his fingers feel this good, how fabulous will sex be?

"Fuuuck," he groans, watching me come apart, and the raw desire in his expression pushes me over the edge.

I cry out as pleasure ripples through me. It's different from the first time. Deeper. More intense. I ride his fingers through the aftershocks, not caring how desperate I must look, how wanton.

When the car finally slows, I'm still catching my breath.

"We're here," Kevin says, withdrawing his fingers. His voice is rough with barely-contained lust.

I look out the window. A sleek building rises into the sky. The kind of building I've walked past a hundred times without ever imagining I'd go inside.

I'm in a daze as we walk through the lobby. The doorman nods like everything is perfectly normal—like disheveled girls in ball gowns stumble through here at midnight all the time. Maybe they do. I'm too sex-drunk to care.

The elevator ride to the top floor takes forever. Kevin keeps his hand on my lower back, a steady point of contact, but he doesn't kiss me. Doesn't touch me beyond that. Like he's barely holding himself together.

When the doors open, I step out into... another world.

The penthouse is stunning. Floor-to-ceiling windows that frame the city skyline. Modern furniture and a kitchen bigger than my entire apartment.

I don't belong here.

The thought arrives unbidden. This is a world I'll never actually be part of. After tonight, the carriage turns back into a pumpkin and I go back to being a broke college student who got one wild night with a man way out of her league.

Then Kevin is kissing me again, and I stop caring about everything but his mouth.

He walks me backward through the penthouse, his lips never leaving mine, until we reach a doorway. His bedroom.

Every nerve ending tingles.

I'm about to lose my virginity to this gorgeous, older man who makes me feel things I didn't know I could feel.

And I still haven't told him.

What if he doesn't want to deal with someone who has no idea what she's doing? What if he wants experienced? What if—

He kisses me again, deep and claiming, and I stop spiraling.

The massive bed with dark sheets looms in front of us. Everything feels suddenly, terrifyingly real.

"Wait," I say, and my voice comes out shakier than I'd like.

Kevin stops immediately. Concern floods his expression. "What's wrong?"

"Nothing's wrong. I..." I inhale slowly, trying to gather my courage. Hands trembling. "I need to tell you something."

"You can tell me anything." He cups my face gently, thumbs stroking my cheekbones.

I can do this. I can be brave. I kissed him first in that boutique. I can do this too.

"I've never done this before." The words tumble out in a rush—clumsy and panicked and completely lacking in the sexy sophistication I was hoping for. "Any of this. Like, at all. I'm a virgin."

There. I said it. Now he's going to politely call me an Uber and I'll die of embarrassment.

His expression shifts in surprise, but he doesn't pull away. "Jennifer—"

"I know I should have told you earlier," I barrel on before I can lose my nerve, "and I know you probably don't want to deal with someone who has no experience, but I want this, I've been thinking about it all day, and I'm ready, I promise, I'm just nervous because I have no idea what I'm doing and what if I'm terrible at it or what if—"

He silences me with a kiss.

It's tender and it makes my chest ache. Nothing like the desperate, hungry kisses from before. This is... soft. Reassuring.

"Princess," he murmurs against my lips. "We don't have to do anything you're not ready for."

"But I am ready." I grip his jacket like it's the only thing keeping me upright. "I'm just warning you that I might be awkward or do something wrong or—"

"Stop." He presses his forehead against mine. "Anything you do is going to be perfect. And knowing that I get to be your first..." His voice drops lower. Rougher. "That you're choosing me for this... Fuck, that's the hottest thing I've ever heard."

"Really?" My voice is small. Uncertain.

"Really." He trails his fingers down my neck, and I shiver. "I'm going to make sure your first time is everything it should be. I'm going to take care of you."

The way he says it makes my throat tight.

"Promise?" I whisper.

"I promise." He kisses me gently, then deeper, coaxing my mouth open. "Now let me show you how good this can be."

As he kisses me, the nervousness doesn't disappear completely. But it transforms into anticipation. Trust. And the wild, reckless hope that this might be the start of something real.

Chapter 5

He leads me further into the bedroom and turns me around gently. His fingers find the zipper at the back of my dress, and the sound of it lowering seems impossibly loud in the quiet room. Each tooth separating feels like a countdown to the moment he sees all of me.

"Tell me if you want to stop," he murmurs against my neck. "At any point. We can stop."

"I don't want to stop," I breathe.

The dress falls away. It pools at my feet in a whisper of peach fabric, and suddenly I'm standing in my pale pink lace bra and panties.

Every instinct screams at me to cover myself. To cross my arms over my stomach, hide the soft parts I usually bury under oversized sweaters. He's behind me, which means he's looking at my back, my ass, all the angles I can't see in my own mirror. What if there's a weird bump I don't know about? What if my underwear is riding up wrong? What if he's comparing me to other women—women who knew what they were doing, whose bodies weren't soft in all the wrong places?

"Christ," Kevin breathes.

I brace for rejection… it doesn't come.

His hands wrap around my hips, and I can feel the heat of his palms through the thin lace. "You're stunning."

Oh.

I turn to face him, fighting the urge to suck in my stomach. The hunger in his eyes makes me feel powerful despite everything—despite my inexperience, despite the voice in my head cataloging every flaw. He's looking at me like I'm beautiful.

Maybe I don't need to know what I'm doing. Maybe I just need to feel.

I reach for his jacket. He helps me push it off his shoulders, and it falls to the floor with a soft thump. My fingers are clumsy with his tie—I've never undone a man's tie before, and apparently it's harder than it looks in movies.

He covers my hands with his. "Let me."

I watch as he loosens the tie and pulls it free, then starts on the buttons of his shirt. Each inch of skin revealed makes my mouth go dry. He's all muscle and smooth skin, the kind of body that comes from hard work at a gym.

When the shirt falls away, I can't help but reach out and touch him. His muscles jump under my fingers like he's been shocked.

"You can touch me anywhere you want," he says. His voice is rough. Strained.

So I do. I explore his chest, his abs, feeling the hard planes of his body. When I brush my fingers over the trail of dark hair below his navel, he inhales sharply. He's being patient, letting me explore at my own pace. But I can see the tension in his shoulders. The way his hands are fisted at his sides.

He's holding back. For me.

"I want to see all of you," I whisper. The words come out bolder than I feel.

His expression darkens. He reaches for his belt, and I watch as he undoes it, then the button of his pants, then the zipper. When he pushes them down along with his boxers, I stop breathing.

Um...

Oh wow.

He's big. Really big. And hard—so hard and curved upward. I have absolutely no idea how that's supposed to fit inside me. The logistics seem... improbable.

"Jennifer," he says gently. I realize I've been staring at his cock. Openly. Like a complete idiot. "We'll go slow. I'll make sure you're ready."

I nod, not trusting my voice. My gaze keeps drifting back to his cock like it's a magnet. Is that rude? Should I be making eye contact instead?

He guides me to the bed. When I sit on the edge, he kneels in front of me and removes my heels one at a time. His lips brush the instep of each foot, and I shiver.

"Lie back," he murmurs.

I do, propping myself up on my elbows so I can watch him. I want to see everything. I want to remember every detail.

He hooks his fingers in my panties and pulls them down slowly. The cool air hits my heated skin, and I'm suddenly, completely exposed to him. Every instinct screams at me to close my legs, but I force myself to stay open. Vulnerable.

What if he doesn't like what he sees? What if I'm different from other women? What if—

"So beautiful," he murmurs, cutting off my spiral. He kisses up the inside of my thigh, and each press of his lips sends sparks through me. "And so wet for me."

His mouth reaches my pussy, and I gasp in delight as his tongue glides through my folds. Pleasure spreads through me like nothing I've ever felt. His tongue is soft and wet and he's looking at me while he does it, and I don't know what to do with my hands or my hips or my face—

The questions dissolve when his tongue circles my clit.

"Kevin," I moan. My head thrashes against the pillow as he sucks on the bundle of nerves.

Should I be quieter? Louder? Am I supposed to give him feedback? I thread my fingers through his hair without thinking, then immediately wonder if that's too aggressive. But he groans against me in obvious pleasure.

He slides one finger inside me while his mouth works my clit, and I nearly levitate off the bed.

"That's it," he encourages. His voice vibrates against my sensitive skin. "Come for me, Princess."

Am I supposed to be able to come on command? I think frantically. Is that a thing people can do? What if I can't—

He curls his finger, hitting a spot I didn't know existed, and I stop thinking entirely.

"Ohhhh god!" I cry out as pleasure crashes through me. It's more intense than in the car, more intense than the balcony, more intense than anything I've ever given myself. I'm shaking as he works me through it, his tongue gentling as the waves subside.

Holy shit.

Is it always this good? Are all my friends having orgasms like this and not telling me?

When I can finally breathe again, I look down to find him watching me with dark, hungry eyes. His chin is wet. From me.

"You taste incredible," he says.

That's so dirty. My face flames, but my core clenches with desire.

He moves up my body with soft kisses until his mouth claims mine. I can taste myself on his tongue, and it's oddly hot.

"I need you," I whisper against his lips. And I do. I need to know what it feels like. I need to stop being the girl who doesn't know.

He reaches behind me, and his fingers work the clasp of my bra. It falls away, and now I'm completely naked. Completely exposed. I resist the urge to cover my breasts with my arms—they're not big, not impressive, definitely not the kind you see in magazines or porn—but he cups them like they're perfect, brushing his thumbs over my nipples.

"So beautiful," he murmurs.

"You keep saying that." My voice comes out breathless. "But I'm not."

He stills. Meets my eyes with an intensity that pins me in place. "You're gorgeous and perfect exactly the way you are. Don't ever let anyone tell you otherwise."

The words crack me open. I'm gorgeous.

He dips his head and takes one nipple into his mouth. The sensation shoots straight to my core—a direct line of pleasure I didn't know existed. He sucks gently, then harder, and I'm writhing beneath him, all my self-consciousness forgotten.

"Please," I whimper.

"Please what?" He switches to my other breast. "Tell me what you need."

"I need you inside me." The words come out desperate. I barely recognize my own voice. "I need to feel you."

He groans and positions himself between my legs. I feel his cock pressing against my entrance.

"If it hurts, tell me," he says. "We'll stop."

"Okay," I whisper.

He pushes the tip in slowly.

A gasp escapes me. It's a burning stretch, different from his fingers.

"Breathe," he reminds me. I realize I've been holding my breath.

I exhale. He pushes in a little more, and the burn intensifies. My fingers dig into his shoulders, probably leaving marks.

Is this normal? Is it supposed to hurt this much? What if something's wrong with me?

"You're doing so good," he murmurs and kisses my neck. "Just a little more."

He slides in another inch, and I whimper. It's too much. He's too big. I was right—the logistics are impossible.

"I know, Princess. I know." He stills completely, giving me time to adjust. "You're taking me so well."

Warmth blooms in my chest from the praise. I focus on that—on his voice, on his patience, on the way he's looking at me like I'm precious.

"More," I manage. I rock my hips experimentally, and—oh. That's... better. The burn is fading, replaced by a pleasurable fullness.

He groans and sinks in further. Suddenly he's all the way inside me. Fully seated. I feel impossibly stretched in ways

I didn't know I could be stretched. It's overwhelming and strange and somehow exactly right.

"Fuck," he breathes. "You feel amazing. So tight. So perfect."

He's not moving. He's waiting for me. I shift my hips again, testing, and pleasure sparks through the fullness.

Oh. That's what everyone's been talking about.

"Okay?" he asks. His voice is strained, like it's taking everything in him to stay still.

"Yes," I moan. "More. Please."

He pulls out slowly—the drag making me gasp—and when he pushes back in, my eyes flutter closed.

It's incredible.

He does it again, and I press my feet against the mattress so I can push up toward him. We find a rhythm together—him thrusting, me meeting him—and the pleasure builds in layers with each stroke.

"Tell me what you need," he groans.

"Faster," I gasp. "Please."

He picks up the pace, and I rock my hips to match. I'm learning. Figuring it out. Each angle feels slightly different, and I experiment—tilting my hips, wrapping my legs around him, arching my back—and apparently I'm not terrible at this because he's groaning and his rhythm is getting ragged.

He slides a hand between us and rubs my clit in time with his thrusts.

I cry out. The dual sensation—him filling me, his fingers on my clit—is almost too much.

"That's it," he encourages, thrusting harder. "Come for me. Let me feel it."

One sharp thrust hits a magical spot deep inside me, and I shatter. Pleasure consumes me, and I cry out his name as I clench around him.

"Fuck, yes," he growls. His rhythm falters but doesn't stop. He fucks me through my orgasm, extending the pleasure until I'm writhing and whimpering beneath him.

When I finally come down, I'm trembling. Gasping. But he's still hard inside me.

"Again," he says. It's not a question. "I want you to come again."

"I can't," I protest weakly. My whole body feels like jelly.

"You can." He pulls out completely—and I feel the loss like a physical thing—then he commands, "Get on your hands and knees. I want that lovely ass in the air."

I roll over on shaky limbs and position myself. Hands and knees. Ass up.

Oh fuck.

I've seen this position in videos. Late at night, volume low, feeling vaguely guilty about the whole thing. But experiencing it firsthand is nothing like watching it on a screen.

I feel exposed. Vulnerable. Ridiculous. He can see everything from back there. Every inch of me is on display.

What if I look weird? What if—

He runs his hands over my ass and squeezes gently. "So fucking beautiful."

Okay. Maybe not ridiculous.

Before I can spiral further, he sinks back into me, and from this angle, he feels even bigger. I cry out in delight.

He stills. "Too much?"

"No." I push back against him. "Don't stop."

He pulls out and drives back in, hitting a spot that makes my toes curl. Every thrust sends pleasure shooting up my spine. I bury my face in the pillow to muffle my moans.

"Fuck," he groans, grasping my hips. "You feel incredible."

He pulls me back to meet his thrusts, and the sound of skin slapping against skin fills the room. It's obscene. And turns me on even more.

"Touch yourself," he commands. "I want to feel you come on my cock again."

Touch myself. While he's inside me.

My face flames. I've done this alone, obviously, but with an audience? With him watching?

But I rest on one elbow so I can reach between my legs anyway, because apparently I've lost all shame tonight, and when my fingers find my clit—

"That's my good princess," he praises, his voice rough. "Taking my cock so well. Coming for me like you were made for it."

His words push me over the edge. I come with a muffled scream, clenching around him as pleasure whites out my vision. I'm seeing actual stars. Or maybe I'm dying. Both seem possible.

"Fuck, Jennifer," he groans.

But he still hasn't come. He keeps thrusting, fucking me through the pleasure, and I'm a trembling mess when he suddenly pulls out and flips me onto my back.

I barely have time to catch my breath before he's pushing inside me again.

"I want to see your face," he says, bracing himself above me. "I want to watch you come apart for me one more time."

"I can't," I whimper as my body shakes. "I can't come again."

"Yes, you can." He fucks me with long, deep strokes that make my eyes roll back. "You're going to come one more time. And then I'm going to fill this sweet pussy and breed it."

Breed.

The word shocks through me like electricity. That's so dirty. So wrong. I shouldn't be turned on by it—the practical implications, the recklessness, the sheer caveman energy of it.

My pussy clenches around him anyway. Apparently my body doesn't care about wrong.

He hooks one of my legs over his shoulder, and the new angle makes him hit that wonderful spot inside me.

"There it is," he says with satisfaction. "Right there."

He pounds into that spot relentlessly, and I didn't think it was possible, but I'm climbing toward another orgasm.

"Fuck, fuck, fuck." My vocabulary has been reduced to one word.

"That's it, Princess." He rubs my clit with his thumb. "Come for me like a good girl so I can breed you."

I explode.

This time the ecstasy rips through my entire body, all the way from my scalp to my toes. I'm shaking and crying out nonsense, completely lost.

"Fuck, yes," he groans, and then he buries himself to the hilt and stills. I feel him pulse inside me, feel the hot rush of him filling me with ropes of sticky cum. His whole body shudders as he empties himself.

I can feel every twitch. Every pulse. He's coming inside me, marking me, and some primal part of my brain that I didn't know existed is screaming yes, this, more.

When he's finally done, he collapses beside me and pulls me onto his chest. I melt into him, completely boneless, and rest my ear against his heart. It's racing as fast as mine.

"Holy shit," I breathe.

He laughs, the sound rumbling through his chest. "Yeah. Holy shit."

I did it. I actually did it. And he didn't look at me with disappointment. And I came—four times—and apparently I'm not terrible at sex after all.

I shift slightly and wince from a twinge between my legs.

"Sore?" he asks, immediately concerned.

"A little." I smile against his chest. "But in a good way."

He kisses my forehead. "Stay here. I'll get a cloth to clean you up."

He disappears into the bathroom, and I lie there in his massive bed, staring at the ceiling, trying to process what happened tonight. The room smells like sex and his cologne. A combination of us.

He returns with a warm washcloth and cleans between my thighs with a gentleness that makes my eyes sting. It's such a small thing. Such a tender thing. Taking care of me after.

"Thank you," I whisper.

"For what?"

"For making my first time incredible."

He tosses the washcloth aside and climbs back into bed, pulling me against his chest. "Thank you for trusting me with it."

His breathing is already evening out, his arm heavy across my waist. "Mine," he murmurs, and it sounds like a promise.

I lie there in the dark, listening to his heartbeat slow, and feel the weight of everything that just happened pressing down on my chest.

What did I just do?

Chapter 6

I WAKE UP DISORIENTED.

The room is dark except for the city lights filtering through floor-to-ceiling windows. For a moment, I don't remember where I am. The sheets are too soft. The bed is too big. Everything smells like cedar and amber and—

Then I feel the weight of Kevin's arm across my waist. The soreness between my legs. The sticky residue of what we did dried on my inner thighs.

I lost my virginity to a man I met four days ago.

A man who paid me fifteen thousand dollars to be his date. A man who's fourteen years older than me and lives in a penthouse I couldn't afford in a hundred lifetimes. A man who probably does this—finds some young, desperate girl, makes her feel special, fucks her, and moves on.

No. Stop. He said I was his. He said he'd never felt like this before. He said—

Men say things during sex. Everyone knows that. The dirty talk, the "you're mine," the "I want to breed you"—that's heat-of-the-moment stuff. It doesn't mean anything in the harsh light of 3 a.m.

My chest tightens. I can't breathe properly in this room that smells like him and sex. Every surface screams you don't belong and I can't think straight with his arm around my waist making me feel things I'm not supposed to feel this fast.

I need air. I need space. I need to think without his body pressed against mine, reminding me of all the ways he touched me.

I carefully extract myself from under his arm, trying not to wake him. He stirs, makes a soft sound, but doesn't open his eyes. In sleep, he looks younger. Less intimidating. Almost vulnerable.

Don't, I tell myself. Don't romanticize this.

I don't know where my panties and bra ended up. Somewhere on his bedroom floor or kicked under the bed. I don't care. He can throw them away. I find my dress pooled on the floor where it fell and pull it on with shaking hands. The zipper catches halfway up my back, but I manage to wrestle it closed enough to be decent.

I'm looking for my heels when his voice cuts through the darkness.

"Jennifer?"

I freeze. Pulse hammering in my ears.

"What are you doing?" His voice is rough with sleep. Confused.

I turn to find him sitting up in bed. The sheets pool around his waist, and even now—even in the middle of this panic spiral—my body responds to the sight of him. The broad chest. The mussed hair. The way his eyes are trying to focus on me in the darkness.

"I need to go," I say. My voice comes out wrong. Too high. Too tight.

He's out of bed immediately, pulling on his boxers as he crosses to me. "What's wrong? Did I hurt you?"

"No. I—" I can't look at him. If I look at him, I'll remember the way he tenderly cleaned me up, and I'll lose my nerve. "I need to leave."

"Talk to me." He reaches for my hands, but I step back. A pained expression flashes across his face—or maybe confusion—and I hate that I'm the one causing it. "Please, Princess. Tell me what's wrong."

Don't call me that. Don't be sweet. Don't make this harder.

"Everything happened so fast." The words tumble out before I can stop them. "We met and I came to your home and we had sex and you're paying me and I don't know what I'm doing. I don't know if this is real or if I'm a—a convenient distraction for you, and I can't—"

My voice cracks. I press my hand to my mouth to stop the flood.

He's quiet for a long moment. I can see him fighting the urge to argue, to convince, to pull me back into bed and make me forget why I'm scared. Instead, he exhales slowly.

"Okay," he says quietly. "Let me call you a car."

"I can get an Uber—"

"Please." His voice cracks slightly on the word. "Let me do this one thing."

I nod because I don't trust my voice.

He pulls out his phone. His jaw is tight as he types, and I can see his hand trembling slightly. When he's done, he looks at me with an expression of hurt and hope all tangled together.

"Fifteen minutes," he says.

The silence between us is suffocating. I want to explain, to apologize, to take it all back and climb into his arms, but I don't know how to put this feeling into words. The terror that he's too good to be true. The certainty that I'll wake up tomorrow and realize this was all some elaborate dream, or worse, some game I didn't know I was playing.

"I'll wait downstairs," I whisper.

"Jennifer—"

"Please. I need to go."

He nods slowly. The pain in his eyes makes my chest ache, but I can't stay here. Not right now. Not when I can't tell the difference between what I want and what I'm terrified of wanting.

I grab my heels and he follows me to the living room while I collect my clutch that somehow ended up in the entryway. I don't put the heels on and hold them against my chest like a shield. When I reach for the door handle, he's suddenly there beside me.

"Whatever you need," he says quietly. "Whatever you decide. I just—" He stops. Swallows hard. "I don't regret tonight. I need you to know that."

"I don't either," I whisper. And it's true. Even in the middle of this panic, I don't regret it. That might be the scariest part.

"Then why does it feel like you're running away from me?"

Because I am. Because I'm terrified of how much I want this—want him—and I don't know how to want something this badly without bracing for it to be ripped away.

"I need to think," I manage.

He nods. He cups my face gently, tilting it up toward his. His thumb brushes across my cheekbone with devastating tenderness.

"Okay," he says. No arguments. No guilt trips. Just acceptance.

He kisses my forehead softly, and it makes my heart crack open in ways I wasn't prepared for.

When he opens the door for me, I make it to the elevator before the tears start.

The lobby is empty except for the night doorman, who nods at me as I pass. I wonder what he thinks—a girl in a wrinkled evening gown at three in the morning, mascara probably smeared, hair a disaster, carrying her heels like she's fleeing a crime scene. I'm sure he's seen worse. This building probably has a revolving door of women doing the exact same walk of shame.

Is that what I am? Another girl leaving Kevin Locke's penthouse at 3 a.m.?

I sink onto a cold bench near the entrance. The chill seeps through the fabric of my dress, and I shiver. I can still smell him on my skin. Still feel the soreness between my legs.

My phone buzzes. I pull it out, expecting a text from Kevin—an apology, or a goodbye.

Instead, it's a notification from my banking app.

Deposit: $15,000.00

I stare at the number until my eyes blur.

That's real. That's sitting in my account right now. Proof that tonight actually happened.

But looking at it confuses me. Was this transactional? How do I separate the money from the man? How do I know if what happened in his bed was real or part of some arrangement I didn't fully understand?

My phone buzzes again. A text this time.

Ella: You up? I just got home from the worst date ever and need to vent.

I don't think. I call her.

She answers on the first ring. "Oh thank god. I need to tell you about this guy who spent the entire night talking about his crypto portfolio and then tried to explain NFTs to me like I'm five—"

"I had sex with him," I blurt out.

Silence.

"Ella?"

"I'm sorry, WHAT?!"

"The guy. Kevin. The one who hired me for the gala." I press my free hand against my eyes. "We had sex."

"Jennifer." I hear movement on her end. She's probably sitting down hard on her couch. "Okay. Okay. Start from the beginning. Tell me everything."

So I do. The shopping. The boutique kiss. The gala. Harrison and his snide comments. The balcony. The car. Coming back to his penthouse and telling him I was a virgin.

"Wait," Ella interrupts. "You told him you were a virgin and he still—"

"He was careful, El. Gentle." My voice breaks. "He made me feel... I don't know. Safe. Precious. Like I mattered."

"So what happened? Why are you sitting in the lobby?"

"I panicked." I swipe at my eyes with the back of my hand. "I woke up and everything hit me at once. How crazy it is. What if he does this all the time? What if I'm another stupid girl who fell for the penthouse and the money and the pretty words?"

"Did he pressure you? Did you feel like you had to?"

"No. God, no." That much I'm certain of. "He kept asking if I was sure. He said we could stop whenever I wanted. He was... Ella, he was perfect. That's the problem. Nobody's that perfect."

"And the money? Did he pay you?"

"It's in my account right now. But that was for the gala—I earned that before we..." I swallow hard. "Everything after the gala was my choice."

"So why aren't you still in his bed?"

The question hangs there. The real question beneath all my spiraling.

"Because I'm scared," I admit. "He's older and richer and so far out of my league. And I barely know him. What if this is some fantasy for him? What if I'm another girl he'll get bored with in a month or two?"

"Did he say that?"

"No. But someone at the gala implied it. That he has a pattern."

"And you believe some random asshole at a party?"

"I don't know what to believe," I whisper. "I don't know how to trust this."

Ella pauses. When she speaks again, her voice is softer. "Okay. What do you want? What do you actually want?"

I look toward the elevators. The doors are closed, waiting. I could go back up. I could go back to him.

Or I could leave. Get in the car when it arrives. Go back to my crappy apartment and pretend tonight never happened.

"I want him," I whisper. The words feel like a confession. "I know it's crazy. But Ella... when I'm with him, I feel like myself for the first time since Mom and Dad died. Like I'm allowed to want things."

"This seems like an easy choice to me."

I press my hand against my chest, trying to ease the tightness there. "Can this be real?"

"The hell if I know, but you won't know if you run."

Headlights appear through the glass doors. The car.

I watch it pull up to the curb.

"Ella?"

"Yeah?"

"Thank you."

"Go get him, babe."

I hang up. The doorman is already moving toward the entrance, ready to open it for me.

"Wait," I say.

He pauses and looks at me.

"I don't need the car anymore."

He nods professionally and steps outside to speak to the driver. The car pulls away.

I stand up. My legs are shaky as I walk toward the elevators. The doorman comes back quickly and holds the door open for me without comment. He probably thinks I forgot something upstairs.

I didn't forget anything. I almost left everything behind.

The elevator ride feels endless. My heart pounds with each floor that ticks by on the digital display. What if he's asleep? What if he's angry that I left? What if he decided while I was gone that I'm too young, too messy, too much trouble?

I walk down the hall on unsteady legs. What am I going to say? "Sorry I panicked and ran, I'm back now"? That's pathetic. He deserves better than pathetic. He deserves someone who doesn't bolt at the first sign of real emotion.

But I'm here. I came back. That has to count for something.

I try the door handle and it opens.

He left it unlocked. Even after I fled. Even after I said I needed to leave. He left the door unlocked in case I changed my mind.

That small gesture—that quiet faith—makes my throat tight.

I push the door open quietly. The penthouse is dark except for a wedge of light spilling from the bedroom. I set my clutch on the couch, leave my heels beside it, and follow the light like a beacon.

He's sitting on the edge of the bed. Head in his hands. Shoulders slumped in a way I've never seen—none of the confidence, none of the control. He looks devastated.

Because I left.

"Kevin," I whisper.

His head snaps up. For a moment, he stares at me like he can't believe I'm real, like he's afraid I'll disappear if he blinks.

"You came back," he says. His voice is rough.

"I'm sorry." The words catch in my throat. "I panicked. Everything happened so fast and I—I didn't know how to handle it. I've never felt like this before and it scared me and I thought—"

He's across the room in three strides, and then his hands are cupping my face, his eyes searching mine. "Don't apologize. Don't ever apologize for needing space." His thumbs brush away tears I didn't realize were falling. "I was afraid I'd pushed you too far. That I'd ruined this."

"You didn't ruin anything." I cover his hands with mine. "I was terrified of how much I wanted this. Of how fast I fell."

Raw emotion flickers in his eyes. "I've been terrified since the moment you walked into that café," he admits. "I've never felt like this before. It's fucking terrifying."

"I talked to my friend Ella," I say. "She asked me what I wanted."

"And?" His voice is barely above a whisper.

"I want to stay." I step closer, pressing myself against him. "Not because you paid me. Not because of the penthouse or the shopping or any of that. I want to stay because of you."

Fierce possessiveness flashes in his eyes. "The money—"

"I'm keeping it. I earned it at the gala." I press my palm against his chest, feeling his heart race beneath my fingers. "But everything after that? That wasn't part of any deal. That was me choosing you."

He makes a sound low in his throat—relief and hunger—and then he's kissing me. Different from before. Slower. Deeper. Like he's convincing himself I'm real.

When he pulls back, his forehead rests against mine. "Stay," he whispers. "Please stay."

"I'm not going anywhere," I promise. "No more running."

He reaches around and pulls the zipper of my dress down slowly. It falls away for the second time tonight, and I'm standing in front of him naked.

But this time, there's no nervousness. No uncertainty. No voice in my head cataloging my flaws.

This time, I'm choosing to be brave instead of scared.

He lifts me easily, and I wrap my legs around his waist as he carries me to the bed. When he lays me down, it's gentle.

"I thought I lost you," he murmurs against my skin, pressing kisses along my collarbone.

"You didn't." I thread my fingers through his hair. "I'm right here."

He makes love to me differently this time. Slower. Sweeter. Every touch deliberate, every kiss lingering. Like he's convincing himself I'm staying.

When I come, it's with his name on my lips and his eyes locked on mine. No hiding. No looking away.

After, he pulls me against his chest. I fit perfectly in the curve of his body. I was made to be here.

"No more running," he says softly.

"No more running," I agree.

I fall asleep to the sound of his heartbeat, and for the first time in three years, I feel like I'm home.

Chapter 7

I WAKE UP WARM. Really warm. There's an arm draped across my waist—heavy, possessive—and breath against the back of my neck. Kevin. His skin pressed against mine.

Holy shit, this is real.

I didn't dream it. I actually came back here. I actually let him—

God, I can still feel where he was inside me. A dull ache between my thighs that makes me squeeze them together involuntarily.

"You're thinking too loud," Kevin murmurs against my hair, and I nearly jump out of my skin.

"How long have you been awake?" I turn in his arms. He's watching me with that intense focus, the kind that makes my stomach flip and my brain short-circuit simultaneously. Like he's memorizing every freckle on my body.

"A while." He brushes hair back from my cheek, fingers gentle. "Couldn't stop watching you sleep. Kept thinking you might disappear again."

My chest tightens. The vulnerability in his voice makes me melt.

"I said I'd stay."

"I know. But I almost lost you." His hand slides down my side, settles on my hip. His thumb traces circles that make me shiver.

"I came back."

"You did." There's a fierceness in his eyes. "Any regrets?"

Last night I gave this man my virginity. Let him do things to me I'd only read about. And I loved it.

"None." The word comes out breathless. "I want you. I want this. Even though it's crazy and too fast and I should probably be freaking out more than I am."

"Should you?" He rolls me onto my back in one smooth motion. Settles between my thighs before I can think. I can feel him against me—hard already, pressing against my pussy.

Oh. Oh god. My hips shift without permission.

"Say it again." His voice has dropped into that commanding tone.

"I want you." The words tumble out.

"Again." He rocks forward. The friction sends a jolt through me and I gasp.

"I want you." How am I already wet? "And I want—" The words stick in my throat. Can I say this? Out loud? In daylight?

Fuck it.

"I want you to breed me."

He groans like I've punched him. Then he's pushing inside me slowly. The stretch is—god, it's intense. Not as sharp as the first time but I feel every inch. My body's still learning to take him and I'm hyper-aware of every nerve ending.

"You feel incredible." He growls. "So tight. So fucking perfect."

I moan and push against him, trying to get him to fuck me.

"Please," I whimper.

Then he starts moving—deep thrusts that hit an amazing spot inside me—and coherent thought evaporates.

"Oh fuck." My back arches off the bed.

"That's it." He watches my face like he's cataloging every reaction as the pressure builds in my core. "Let me see you."

"Kevin—" I don't know what I'm asking for.

"You're mine, Jennifer." His pace picks up, and every thrust makes stars sparkle along the corners of my vision from pleasure. "Say it."

"I'm yours." The words come easy because they're true.

"Say you're mine." He drives in harder. "Mine to fill. Mine to keep."

Oh god. The possessive tone shouldn't be this hot. I clench around him involuntarily and we both groan.

"I'm yours." I'm babbling now. "All yours."

"Mine to breed."

The word sends electricity shooting through me. Last night when he said it, I didn't expect to love it this much. But now? Now I want it. I want it so badly it scares me a little.

"Yes." My voice comes out as a whimper. "Breed me."

His rhythm stutters. "Fuck."

I dig my nails into his shoulders. Some bold, reckless part of me takes over. "I want you to knock me up. I want to carry your baby."

Am I insane? I might be insane. Twenty-one years old, asking a man to get me pregnant. But I don't care. I want his baby.

"Jesus." He buries his face in my neck. His hips snap forward harder. Faster. "Do you mean that? Really mean it?"

"Yes." I rock up to meet him, chasing the pleasure. "I want you to get me pregnant."

He lifts his head. His eyes are dark, almost black with lust. "I'll give you anything you want, Princess. Anything."

I pull him down for a kiss—messy, desperate. "I'm going to let you breed me every day," I breathe against his mouth. "As many times as you want."

He makes this noise—wounded, broken—and his hand finds my clit. Rubs in firm circles while he fucks me.

"You want me to fill this sweet pussy every day?" His voice has gone rough. Ragged. "Keep you full of my cum?"

"Yes." The pleasure builds until it's unbearable. "I need your cum every day."

I sound like a porn star. Who is this person? Where did she come from?

"Fuck." His rhythm goes erratic. "Come for me first, Princess. Then I promise I'll give you so much cum you'll be dripping for days."

His thumb presses harder on my clit and I shatter. The orgasm tears through me—waves of it—and I cry out his name. I'm clenching around him so tight it's almost painful.

"That's it." He groans. "Milk my cock. Take every fucking drop."

He buries himself deep. I feel him pulse. Hot cum flooding into me—so much of it—and the primal part of my brain screams yes. This. This is what I wanted.

We collapse together. Both breathing hard. I can feel his cum leaking out onto the sheets. I feel... claimed. Marked.

"That was..." I can't finish the sentence.

"Yeah." He kisses my temple. "It was."

A laugh bubbles out of me—half hysterical. "I can't believe I said all that. About wanting you to get me pregnant."

"I can't believe how fucking hot it was hearing you say it." He props himself up, looks down at me with tenderness. "You're full of surprises, you know that?"

Heat floods my cheeks. "I don't know where that came from."

"I love it." He traces his fingers down my side. "I love that you're discovering what you want. That you're brave enough to ask for it."

"I'm not brave." The admission slips out. "I'm terrified. But I'm doing it anyway."

"That's what brave is." He kisses me, soft and sweet, a contrast to everything we just did. "Come on. Let's get you cleaned up."

The shower is small for two people, especially when one of them is Kevin's size. But he washes my hair with gentle fingers, soaps every inch of me like I'm precious. When his hand slides between my thighs, I wince.

He freezes. "Too sore?"

"A little." I bite my lip. Should I say this? "But I like it. It reminds me of you. Of what we did."

His eyes go dark again. "Christ, you can't say things like that."

"Why not?"

"Because it makes me want to fuck you again."

"So fuck me again."

Wow, listen to me. I'm a little slutty when I'm turned on. It's great.

He groans, dropping his forehead to mine. "You need time to recover."

"I'm fine."

"Later." A promise. "But right now, you need food."

He wraps me in a towel and finds one of his shirts for me to wear. When I step out of the bathroom—hair wet, drowning in cotton that smells like him—he stares at me like I'm the most beautiful thing he's ever seen.

Which is insane. I look like a drowned rat in a tent.

"What?" I ask, suddenly self-conscious.

"You. In my shirt. In my home." He crosses the room in two strides, pulls me against him. "I could get used to this."

My heart trips over itself. "Yeah?"

"Yeah."

He makes breakfast. I perch on a barstool and watch him crack eggs, chop vegetables, move around the kitchen with the same easy competence he brings to everything. His muscles shift under his t-shirt with each movement and I have to look away before I start drooling.

"You cook?" I ask, mostly to distract myself.

"I have many talents." That devastating half-smile. "You'll discover them all eventually."

Eventually.

The word makes me feel warm. Safe.

We eat in comfortable silence. The omelet is perfect—fluffy, seasoned exactly right. The fruit is fresh. Everything tastes amazing.

"So." He sets down his fork. "About last night. When you came back."

I brace myself. Here it comes. The part where he tells me this was a mistake, we got carried away, maybe we should slow down—

"I realized something."

"What?"

He takes my hand. His thumb brushes across my knuckles.

"I don't want you to leave again. Not tonight. Not tomorrow." His voice drops. "Not ever."

I open my mouth. Nothing comes out.

"Move in with me." The words hang there. His expression is—god, he looks almost nervous. Like he's waiting for me to bolt. "I know it's fast. I know you probably need time to think about it and I'll give you all the time in the world. But last night, sitting in that hallway thinking you were gone—" He stops. Takes a breath. "I don't want to pressure you. If you need to go back to your apartment, I understand. But I want you here. I want to wake up with you every morning."

My brain is screaming. Too fast.

But then I think about sitting in the lobby last night. Realizing I was running from the first good thing that's happened to me in years. The choice I made when I walked back through those doors.

"I can't afford to split rent on a place like this," I hear myself say.

"I'm not asking you to pay rent." His grip on my hand tightens. "I want to take care of you. Let you focus on school."

"That's too much."

"Nothing would be enough." His eyes are intense. "I want to give you everything. Not because you need it. But because I need to. Because taking care of you—" He pauses, like he's searching for words. "It feeds my soul, Jennifer. Being the person you lean on."

I stare at this man. This insane, wonderful, too-good-to-be-true man who's offering me a life I never dared to imagine.

Tears prick my eyes. Shit. I'm not going to cry.

"Why me?" The question comes out wobbly. "You could have anyone. Literally anyone."

He lifts my hand to his lips and presses a kiss to my palm. "Because you kissed me in that boutique like you couldn't help yourself. Because you're genuine and kind and you don't want me for my money." He kisses the pad of my finger. "Because when I'm with you, I feel alive for the first time in years."

"I feel that too." My voice is barely a whisper. "Like everything before you was just... waiting."

"Then let me take care of you."

He kisses another fingertip. Then another. Like he's worshipping me.

My heart is pounding so hard I'm surprised he can't hear it.

"Yes." The word slips out before I can overthink it. "Yes, I'll move in."

The smile that breaks across his face—god. It's like watching the sun come out.

He comes around the counter, pulls me into his arms, kisses me deep and thorough. "You won't regret this," he murmurs against my lips.

"I know." And somehow, impossibly, I mean it.

He laughs—a real laugh, full of joy—and lifts me onto the counter. Steps between my thighs. Slides his hands up my legs, pushing his shirt higher.

"We should celebrate."

"How?" I ask, even though I already know. I can feel his hard cock pressing against my thigh.

"I can think of a few ways." His palm cups me. I'm already wet. Again. Still. "Starting with making you come on this counter."

"Kevin—" A moan. He's sliding two fingers inside me and I can't think. "You said we had to wait."

"I know." He pumps slowly. "But I need you too much. Can't keep my hands off you, Princess."

When he slides his cock inside me, I gasp at the stretch. At the fullness. At the way he fills every empty space inside me.

He fucks me hard and fast while I cling to the counter and wrap my legs around him. While I try to remember who I was before this.

Someone who was running.

Someone who was scared.

But right now, with Kevin's eyes locked on mine, with the promise of a future I never let myself want—

I'm not scared anymore.

I'm home.

Epilogue

ONE YEAR LATER.

I stand in front of the full-length mirror in our bedroom and smooth my hands over my belly. Six months pregnant. The curve is obvious under my dress, impossible to hide even if I wanted to.

I don't want to.

Sometimes I still can't believe this is my life. A year ago, I was broke and desperate. Staring at sixty-three dollars and wondering how to make rent. Creating a profile on a sugar baby website because I'd run out of options.

Now I'm living in a penthouse. Engaged. Pregnant with our daughter.

Our daughter.

She kicks against my palm—hard, like she's annoyed I'm standing still—and I smile.

"Hey, baby girl. Your daddy's going to be home soon."

As if he heard me, the front door opens. "Jennifer? Where are my girls?"

My heart does that stupid flutter thing it always does when I hear his voice. You'd think after a year I'd be used to it.

"Bedroom!" I call back.

He appears in the doorway, still in his suit from work. Tie loosened, hair slightly mussed like he's been running his hands through it. But his face lights up when he sees me.

"There you are." He crosses to me immediately, hands settling on my belly. "How is she today?"

"Active. She's been kicking all afternoon."

As if on cue, a strong kick lands right against his palm. His face transforms with wonder, like he can't quite believe there's a person in there.

"There she is," he murmurs. "Hey, baby. It's Daddy."

I lean back against him. He wraps his arms around me, cradling our daughter through my dress.

"How was work?" I ask.

"Long. I missed you." He kisses my neck and I shiver. "Both of you."

"We missed you too."

I'm on summer break from classes. Going back online in the fall because I don't want to miss anything with the baby. Kevin makes it clear I can take a break from college entirely if I want—says he'll support whatever I decide—but finishing my degree matters to me. It's the one thing that was mine before him. I want to see it through.

He's never once made me feel like my goals are less important than his. That might be the thing I love most about him.

Though I'm also excited to be a mom. More excited than I ever expected. The girl who couldn't afford rent, who ate ramen for dinner and counted quarters for laundry—she's going to be someone's mother. Still wild to think about.

"I have something for you," Kevin says.

"You bought me that new car last week. I don't need anything else."

"It's not that kind of gift." He pulls a small velvet box from his pocket.

My breath catches. We're already engaged—have been for six months, since the day I told him I was pregnant and he dropped to his knees right there in the kitchen, pulled out a ring he'd apparently been carrying for weeks, and proposed through tears. But this box is different. Smaller.

He opens it. Inside is a delicate bracelet with three charms. A tiny heart. Miniature baby shoes. And a calendar charm set to a specific date—our first date. The café.

"Kevin," I breathe. "It's beautiful."

"One charm for each of my girls." He fastens it around my wrist. "And one for the day everything changed."

He doesn't need to say which day. We both know.

I turn in his arms. Kiss him. Pour everything I feel into it—the gratitude, the disbelief, the love that still catches me off guard with its intensity.

"I love you," I whisper against his lips.

"I love you too. Both of you." His hand finds my belly again. "I can't believe this is real sometimes."

"Believe it. Because you're stuck with us now."

"Best fate I could imagine."

He pulls me toward the bed, and I go willingly.

He makes love to me slowly. Worshipping my changing body with his hands and mouth. Telling me I'm stunning. That he's never wanted me more. That he loves the curve of my belly, every change my body is going through to carry our daughter.

I believe him. That's the difference between now and a year ago. I believe him when he says I'm beautiful. When he says I'm his. When he says he loves me.

After, we lie tangled together. His hand rests on my belly, feeling our daughter move.

"Remember when I tried to run?" I ask, tracing patterns on his chest.

His arm tightens around me. "Worst moment of my life."

"I'm glad I came back."

"So am I." He presses a kiss to my forehead. "Best decision you ever made."

"Second best," I correct. "The best was kissing you in that boutique."

He laughs—that deep, rumbling sound I love. "You were so bold. I couldn't believe it."

"I couldn't believe it either. I couldn't help myself. You were standing there looking all sexy." I smile. "Worth the risk."

"I'm glad you thought so." He tilts my face up, kisses me softly. "That kiss changed everything."

"It did." I press my palm against his chest, feeling his heart beat steady and strong. "Now I'm exactly where I'm supposed to be."

Our daughter kicks—hard, like she's agreeing with me.

We both laugh.

"She's going to be brave and incredible like you," he says and pulls me closer.

"No regrets?" I ask. Even though I know the answer.

"Not a single one." He kisses me softly. "You're the best thing that ever happened to me."

"You're the best thing that ever happened to me too." I press my hand over his, both of us cradling our daughter. "I was just surviving before you. Now I'm living."

"We're living," he corrects. "Together."

"Together," I agree.

And as I drift off to sleep in his arms, our daughter safe between us, I think about how one impulsive decision to put myself on a sugar baby website changed everything.

One moment of desperation that led to bravery.

One kiss in a boutique because I couldn't help myself.

One night when I almost ran but came back instead.

Now I have everything I never knew I wanted. Which is wild, because a year ago I didn't even know what I wanted. I was too busy surviving to want anything beyond rent money.

Not bad for a broke college student who just needed to make rent.

Not bad at all.

The End

About Rose Richards

Rose Richards is a spicy writer of age-gap stories that are filthy with a hint of romance. The stories delve into the complexities of lust and desire in forbidden relationships.

www.ingramcontent.com/pod-product-compliance
Lightning Source LLC
Chambersburg PA
CBHW020118310726

48970CB00002B/699